This book belongs to

_____

For Alexandre,
the Rumpelstiltskin in my life.
N.G.

For Oscar and Felix,
Osian and Inigo with love.
P.B.

Rumpelstiltskin

A Grimms tale retold by
NOEL GRAMMONT

Illustrated by
PETER BAILEY

In a far, far away kingdom,

there was a poor miller's daughter who was known for her great beauty.

One day, the King's son came to the mill desperate to catch a glimpse of her. Finding the miller, the Prince spoke with him and saw the lovely girl through an open window. Instantly, he fell in love.

"I wish I could marry your daughter, but my father would never allow a miller's daughter to be my wife. If only she were a princess,"

said the smitten Prince.

"Ah," replied the cunning miller,

"my daughter is far better than any noblewoman,

for she can spin straw into gold!"

"If that is true, the King would certainly let us wed!

Bring her to the palace tomorrow and I shall speak to Him!"

Now the old King was an
unforgiving and *greedy* man.
When the girl was brought to him, he wanted to see proof.

So he brought her to a room filled with straw
and in the corner stood a spinning wheel.

"Work all night if you must," said the King, but if
you do not spin this straw into gold by morning,
you will be put to death!"

The Prince was horrified!
He begged for the girl's life —
but his father ignored him.

"This is how I deal with liars,"

he boomed.

"But it was her father who boasted, not the girl!" cried the Prince.

"Yes," confirmed the King, *"and her death will pain him the most!"*

With that said, the King had the Prince removed
from the palace until the truth would be known.

The poor miller's daughter sat alone not knowing what to do.

Of course she could not spin straw into gold!

Try as she might she could not think how to save her life.

Frightened, she began to cry.

Then all at once there was
a spark of light and with a

pop-sizzle-CRACK!

a little man appeared wearing a colourful
scarf and mismatched stockings.

"Good day, Miss Miller! Why are you sobbing so?"

"I have to spin straw into gold but I do not know how.

If it is not done by morning the King will kill me!" she cried.

"Ah, that is not good; not good at all!" chirped the little man. "Hmm... What will you give me if I do it for you?"

As he spoke, he danced a little jiggle-wiggle
and his stockings magically changed colours.

"My necklace," said the girl.

The little man took the necklace in his leathered hands, squinted at it, and with a nod of approval he hurried it into his pocket.

Smiling, he sprang into a dance, reciting a chant that made the miller's daughter fall into a peaceful slumber.

Go to sleep and have no fear,
I'll spin my spell till morn is near.
Tonight 'tis straw that makes you cry.
Tomorrow gold shall greet your eye.

The funny little man chuckled cheerfully, clapping his hands as the spinning wheel began to turn.

"Whir! Whir! Whir!"

went the wheel, and so it went, until morning.

When the sun rose, all the straw was gone and the room was filled with glistening gold. Then with a spark of light and a

pop-sizzle-CRACK!

the little man was gone!

When the King arrived and saw the gold, he was delighted. He did not understand how the straw had been turned into gold, but it did not matter to him.

Greedy as he was,
he wanted more!

With a click of his fingers, he ordered his guards to bring an even bigger mountain of straw.

"If you value your life you will do as before and spin this straw into gold by morning!"

Turning his back to the girl the King left the
room and locked the door behind him.

Straight away, there was a spark of light and with a
pop-sizzle-CRACK the little man appeared again.

"What will you give me if I spin THIS straw into gold for you?"
he asked.

"I shall gladly give you my ring," answered the young girl.

He took the ring, squinted at it closely and popped it into his pocket.

With a smile he began to dance his jiggle-wiggle, and chanted as before:

Go to sleep and have no fear,
I'll spin my spell till morn is near.
Tonight 'tis straw that makes you cry.
Tomorrow gold shall greet your eye.

The girl fell fast asleep; the spinning wheel began to turn and by morning all the straw was spun into glittering gold.

The King rejoiced. But he wanted *even more gold!*

So, with a click of his fingers,
he demanded his guards to fill the room with
straw right up to the ceiling, and told her,

*"If you can spin this into gold,
I will let you marry my son."*

"She's just a miller's daughter," thought the
King, smiling to himself. *"But with this
girl as my daughter-in-law, my kingdom
will be the richest in the world!"*

When the King left, there was a spark of light,
and with a *pop-sizzle-CRACK* the
little man appeared for the third time.

*"What will you give me
if I spin, once more this
straw into gold?"*
he smiled.

"I have nothing left to give," answered the girl, now with tears in her eyes.

"Then promise me when you are Queen, you will give me your first child."

Not knowing how else to help herself, the miller's daughter agreed. With her promise given, the little man gleefully danced his jiggle-wiggle and chanted once more.

When the King arrived in the morning to find an even *bigger* mountain of glimmering gold, *he gave his blessing for the marriage.*

But soon after the wedding, the greedy old King became ill and passed away. And so it happened that the kind Prince and his radiant bride became *King and Queen.*

One year later,
the Queen gave birth to
a beautiful child and the
entire kingdom celebrated.

She had long forgotten the funny little man until
one day, without notice, there was a flash of light
and with a *pop-sizzle-CRACK*...

... he reappeared. "Now," he said, reaching for the child, *"give me what is mine!"*

Horrified, she held her child to her breast and backed away.

"No! No! Take anything else, all our wealth, but not my child!"

"Why would I want wealth when I can spin straw into gold?" he sneered.

"I want the child to raise as my own."

At that, the Queen fell before him weeping.

She cried so much and so hard that the little man felt sorry for her.

"All right, all right!

If you stop sobbing, I will give you another chance.

You have three days," he said.

*"If you can guess
my name in that time,
you may keep your child."*

The little man giggled.

He knew that his name was so difficult no one could ever guess it!

Then with a flash of light and a *pop-sizzle-CRACK*,

he disappeared just as fast as he had arrived.

The Queen sat up all night trying to remember every name that she had ever heard.

She sent messengers far and wide searching for any unusual names there could be.

They asked everyone they met, the names of all of their children and all their relatives; *they searched everywhere* in the kingdom to find the little man's name.

In the morning the little man returned.

The Queen began to recite all the names, beginning with...

She said all the names the messengers brought her and all
the names she had pondered, one after another; but to every
name the little man politely shook his head and responded,

"No my Queen, that is not my name."

On the second day she sent her messengers even further to distant lands.

"Look harder," she implored them. And they did.

"There must be some strange names out there, and *one of them must be his!"* she told them.

And there were some very strange names!

When the little man returned to the palace,
she tried them all. *"Perhaps your name is
Sizzlefizzle, or Poppy-pop, or Funnypants?"*

He frowned a little but still he answered politely,
"No, my Queen, that is not my name."

The Queen was desperate. She asked her messengers to try even harder, and so they did, searching high and low. Then, at the end of the third day one of the messengers returned with a strange tale.

"As I came to a high mountain in the thickest part of the forest, I saw a little house. Before the house a fire was burning and a little man was jumping up and down singing:

Dance tonight and sing a song.

Because I know before too long

I'll have the child!

Then you will see

Rumpelstiltskin.

That is me!"

Well, you can imagine how relieved and happy the Queen was! She knew it had to be him, she was certain! When the little man returned, he giggled to himself, certain this was the day he would take the royal child home. He bowed politely before the Queen with a big smile and asked,

"Now my Queen, please tell me if you can, what is my name? Eh? Eh?"

"Is it William?" she asked, knowing now that it was not.

"No my Queen," the little man chuckled, imagining how he would raise the royal child. *"That is not my name."*

"Is your name Harry?" she pondered.

"No, no it is not!" said the little man gleefully. He shook his head and smiled a grin from ear-to-ear.

"Is it... let me see... Charles?" she teased.

"No my Queen, that is not my name!" he said, laughing so hard that he had to cover his mouth!

The Queen smiled back at him, raised one eyebrow
and said: *"Well, then, I wonder...*

Rumpelstiltskin?

Hearing his name, the little man stomped his feet in anger!

"How could you know?"

he screamed, red with rage, wiggling his arms over his head,

turning and rolling and then... and then... He simply fell to the

floor weeping and wailing most earnestly, in total despair.

The Queen felt sorry for Rumpelstiltskin.
After all, the little man had helped her many times.
So she thought for a moment and then said,

*"Rumpelstiltskin please –
stay at the palace and entertain us with
your rhymes and good cheer and be
good company to my child."*

And so it happened that Rumpelstiltskin
stayed at the palace and even to this day he
gives everyone a reason to smile with his
jiggle-wiggle and silly stockings!

The end

First published in Great Britain in 2015 by Far Far Away Books and Media, Ltd.
20-22 Bedford Row, London, WC1 R4S

Copyright © 2013
by Far Far Away Books and Media

Illustrations copyright © Peter Bailey, 2013

The moral right of Noel Grammont to be identified as the author and
Peter Bailey to be identified as the illustrator of this work has been asserted.
All rights reserved.

No part of this publication may be reproduced or transmitted
by any means, electronic, mechanical, photocopying or otherwise,
without the permission in writing from the publisher.

ISBN: 978-1-908786-87-6

A CIP catalogue record for this book is available from the British Library

Edited by Richard Trenchard and Vicky Talbot

Printed and bound in Portugal by Printer Portuguesa

All Far Far Away Books can be ordered from
www.centralbooks.com

FAR
FAR
AWAY
BOOKS